The Sweater

Written by *Wendi J. Silvano*

Illustrated by *Guy Francis*

My abuela (that's Spanish for "grandmother")
loves to knit. In her country, she says,
every girl learns to knit when she is young.
But I don't think every girl loves knitting
the way Abuela does.

First thing in the morning,

Abuela pulls out her yellow straw basket

with the pink flowers on it.

Then she reaches in for her knitting and begins.

She knits most of the morning.

She knits after lunch.

She knits in the evening

when she watches TV.

She knits in her bed

before she goes to sleep.

3

You should see the sweaters at our house!

My two brothers and I get new ones

almost every other month.

Abuela knits button-up sweaters for Mamá

and pullover sweaters for Papá.

She even knits sweaters for Mr. Riser

down the street, whose wife died last year.

This morning, when I woke up,

Abuela was in her rocking chair . . .

knitting, of course.

"What are you making this time?" I asked her.

"Oh, just another sweater," she said.

I looked at the odd-shaped sweater.

It was awfully skinny.

"Who is it for?" I asked.

"Someone special," she said.

"Is it for me?"

"No, Anita, not you."

"Is it for Carlito or Raul?"

"No, not them."

"Who, then?" I asked.

"Well . . . you will see," said Abuela.

Abuela knitted all morning.

The sweater got longer and longer.

It reached clear to the floor.

"That doesn't look like a sweater to me,"

I said at lunch.

"It's a sweater," said Abuela.

After lunch, Abuela went back to her knitting.

I kept an eye on her while I practiced the piano.

I watched her while I did my chores.

The sweater kept getting longer and longer.

"Abuela must be teasing me," I thought.

"I'm going to pretend I don't care

who the sweater is for."

Abuela kept knitting, and I kept pretending.

I didn't even look down when the sweater got so long

that I almost stepped on it coming out of the kitchen.

Abuela took it into her room when she went to bed.

I could hear the *klink, klink, klink* of her needles

for a long time.

"She's teasing me!" I said out loud.

In the morning, the sweater reached from Abuela's bed . . .

to her door . . . and out into the hall.

I stormed into her room. "I give up!" I said.

"I have to know who that sweater is for!"

"All right," said Abuela.

"In a few minutes I will be done.

Then you can come with me to deliver the sweater.

But hurry. I don't wait for slowpokes."

Abuela carried the finished sweater

in her straw basket as we hurried down the street.

We knocked on Mr. Riser's door.

"That sweater won't fit him," I whispered to Abuela.

She just smiled.

"Oh, it's perfect!" said Mr. Riser

as Abuela pulled the sweater out of her basket.

"She'll love it!"

"I hope it's long enough," said Abuela.

"I'll go try it on her now," said Mr. Riser.

"Wait here. We'll come back and show you how it looks."

We waited . . . and waited.

I thought I was going to die waiting.

Then, slowly, the door opened, and out came Mr. Riser.

My mouth fell open.

In his arms he carried the longest snake I had ever seen . . .

dressed in a red and blue striped sweater.

"Meet Genie, my pet boa constrictor!" said Mr. Riser.

"A snake!" I said, laughing. "The sweater was for a snake?"

"Of course," said Abuela. "What did you think—that I was teasing you?"

"Not me," I said. "Why would I think that?"